Mouse's magic paints

A first book of colours

Written by Tim Healey
Illustrated by Margaret Chamberlain

PUBLISHED BY THE READER'S DIGEST ASSOCIATION LIMITED

Mouse was very poor and he
lived in a shabby little house. But
he always hoped that something
exciting would happen to him –
and one day it did.
On his birthday the postman
brought a mysterious parcel.

Mouse opened it and found that
a long lost uncle had sent him a
magic paint set.

Mouse tried it out at once. Since
his own clothes were old and
patched, he painted himself a
fine pair of red trousers...

. . . and a splendid yellow shirt. . .

. . . and a magnificent black hat
with a long purple feather.

Dressed in his new finery, Mouse went swaggering off into town. He passed his neighbour, Mrs Hedgehog, who was shivering in her garden.

"Oh Mouse," she complained, "I left my pink shawl on the washing line overnight and the wind must have blown it away. I feel so cold without it."

Quick as a flash, Mouse painted
her a new one.
"But that's amazing!" said Mrs
Hedgehog.
"Mere magic, dear lady,"
Mouse replied.

Mouse walked on to the market square where some jugglers and acrobats were performing before a large crowd.

Suddenly the tightrope snapped,
and one of the acrobats fell with
a bump to the ground.
"Bother!" he exclaimed. "Now
we'll have to stop. We can't do
our tricks without the rope."

Mouse looked at the white cord
and quickly painted in a smart
new one. The acrobats were
astonished. Everyone cheered
Mouse, who bowed low with a
sweep of his hat before
continuing on his way.

Then he saw her – the prettiest
Mouse Lady you could imagine.
She was sitting with a book on a
park bench, with a faraway look
in her eyes.

Mouse fell in love. Madly in love.

"Fair Mouse Lady," he said,
"you seem sad. Is there anything
I can do for you?"
"Oh sir," she replied. "The great
green dragon stole one of my
gloves as I sat here reading."

"Have no fear," Mouse replied,
reaching for his paints. "I'll
paint a new one for you."
But the Mouse Lady interrupted
him.
"You are very kind, sir," she
said. "But I would like my own
glove back."

"Then I will fetch it for you,"
Mouse vowed. He painted
himself a sparkling silver sword,
and hurried into the wood where
the great green dragon lived.

In the wood it was dark. Mouse
felt very alone without his magic
paints. "At least I have my
sword, though," he muttered
under his breath.

"Who dares to bring a sword
into my wood?" boomed a deep
voice. Mouse whirled around
and saw a great green shape
loom up from behind a mossy
rock. It was the dragon. And in
its paw was the Mouse Lady's
blue glove.

"Give me that glove, dragon,"
Mouse called.
"Certainly not, you miserable
little worm!" replied the dragon.
"I'm not a worm," said Mouse.
"I'm a mouse!" and he lunged at
the dragon with his blade.

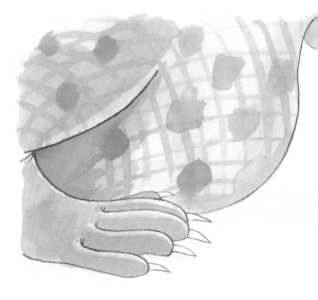

The dragon darted to one side.
"Never touched me!" it
chuckled. But as the dragon
moved, the tip of Mouse's sword
caught the glove.

He had it! Mouse snatched the
glove and ran from the wood,
tossing the sword high over his
shoulder as he went.

As it landed, the sword pierced the dragon's tail – and both sword and dragon vanished in a magical puff of smoke.

Mouse ran back to the Mouse Lady with her glove. She was delighted and promised to go to tea with him. Filled with pride, Mouse rushed home with his paints.

It was such a shabby little house!
Mouse wanted it to look like a
palace for the Lady, and he
painted it red and yellow and
blue and black and purple and
pink and white. He added
touches of green and silver, too,
to remind him of the dragon and
the sword.

Lastly, Mouse painted a gold
ring and placed it on a pale blue
satin cushion. When the Lady
arrived he would ask her to
marry him.

That night Mouse went to bed
very happy.

But when he awoke in the morning his little house was as shabby as ever. All the colours had gone. His fine clothes had vanished – and so too had the satin cushion and ring.

Mouse looked at the calendar. It was his birthday morning. He must have been dreaming!

Mouse heard a knock and, feeling very miserable, he went to his front door. But before he could open it, all his friends burst in. It was a surprise birthday party!

Mouse's friends decked the house
with coloured streamers while he
unpacked his presents. You'll
never guess what he was given:
all the lovely things he'd seen in
his dream!

Then there came another knock
at the door. Mouse answered it,
to find the best surprise of all.
For waiting to join his party were
some jugglers, some acrobats...

. . . and with them a girl who looked just like the Lady in Mouse's dream!

MY WONDERFUL WORDBOX

First Edition Copyright © 1989
The Reader's Digest Association Limited,
Berkeley Square House, Berkeley Square,
London W1X 6AB
Reprinted 1993

® READER'S DIGEST, THE DIGEST and
the Pegasus logo are registered trademarks of
The Reader's Digest Association, Inc.
of Pleasantville, New York, U.S.A.

Printed in Hong Kong

purple